Canary in a cage

An interesting optical illusion is the "canary in the cage." Get a piece of white card about 50 mm (2") square. On one side draw a bird cage, on the other a canary. Fit this card into a slot made in a short piece of stick, preferably round. Roll the stick backwards and forwards between the palms of your hands as fast as you can. The canary will appear to be inside his cage.

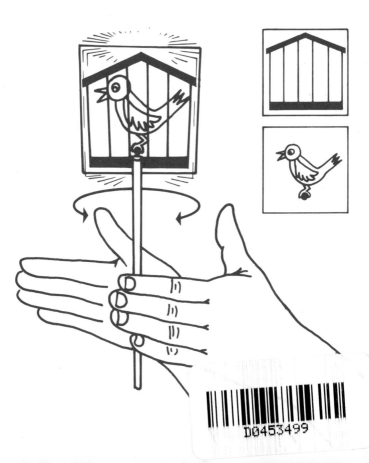

The equipment you will need to carry out the experiments in this book is easy to collect and safe to use. Don't forget a notebook — one of the important things about experimenting is to note what happens so that you can compare it with what happens next time. Scientists always keep a record of their research projects for this reason, so why not do the same?

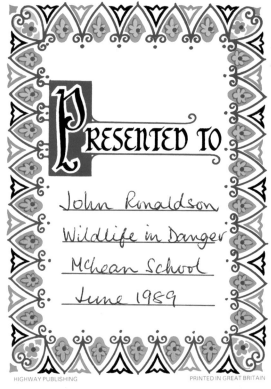

Presented to

John Ronaldson
Wildlife in Danger
McLean School
June 1989

Firs

© L

HIGHWAY PUBLISHING

Light

by JOHN and DOROTHY PAULL

illustrated by DAVID PALMER

Ladybird Books Loughborough

Light

We live on a beautiful and unique planet. Heat and light from the sun brighten and warm huge masses of land and sea day after day, providing very necessary ingredients for life. Occasionally when it rises and sets, the sun fills the sky with dramatic colours.

Sometimes sky colours are affected by freak events. In 1883, a huge volcano erupted on an Indonesian island called Krakotoa. The earth-shattering explosion caused incredible damage to the landscape and threw volcanic ash and rock debris 45 km high into the sky, much of which floated in the atmosphere for many years. The particles of dust made the sunsets around the world unnaturally red for a long period of time. Although not quite so spectacular, sunsets in desert regions often bathe the land in a cloak of red as the sun's rays catch the sand particles blowing in the breeze.

Throughout time man has been fascinated by the sun and its vast source of power over life. Its mystique was felt strongly by primitive tribes who worshipped the sun as a God. As man learned more about his world, he tried to understand and learn more about the sun, and tried many experiments to explain its mysteries.

sunrise at Stonehenge

Where does light come from?

Light is a form of energy and has phenomenal power. It comes to us from a very bright star called the Sun which is an incredible mass of fire suspended in space over 150,000,000km away. The huge flames give off light which travels through vast empty regions of outer space at an unbelievable speed. Light moves so fast from the sun that we couldn't possibly time it with a stopwatch. Measuring its speed confounded many a scientist until the early nineteenth century when its speed was successfully estimated. We now know that it moves at 300,000,000 metres a second! When rays of light leave the blazing sun, they take eight minutes to get here! Mathematicians have worked out another way of describing its speed. One ray of light would go 7½ times around the world in a second. Compare that with Concorde, the supersonic jet!

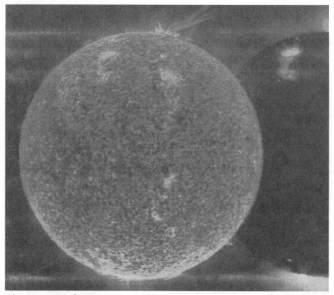

the sun seen from space

There are brighter stars than the sun. You can see them forming beautiful patterns in the night skies. Astronomers using powerful telescopes discovered that our nearest bright star after the sun is Alpha Centaurus and the light from its surface takes over four years to reach us. Four years travelling at 300,000,000m per second! When astronomers look through a telescope at Alpha Centaurus, they see light that left the star four years ago. Other stars are so far away that when we see them twinkling in the dark sky, that light has been travelling so long to reach us, we cannot say for sure that the stars still exist.

What light does

Each day the sun rises in the East and sets in the West. If the sun suddenly exploded, our planet would be plunged into total darkness eight minutes later, and the land and the sea would cool down very quickly. Everything would perish.

What does the sunlight do, apart from helping us to see and to feel warm? It is essential to green plants. They use sunlight in their food making (this process is called photosynthesis), and the plants grow towards the sun so that they can get as much light as possible. You will have seen plants left on kitchen window sills bend at the stem as they lean towards the morning or afternoon sun. If you have a plant like this at home, turn it round the other

way, and check it again after a few days. Notice how the plant grows straight and then turns again towards the sunlight.

Put a small houseplant in the dark for about two weeks (be sure to water it so that it will not die). What happens to its green leaves? The next time you are in the garden, lay down a sheet of old cardboard on the grass and leave it for a few days. What happens to the grass?

Grow some mustard and cress seed on a damp sponge in a saucer, put it in a cardboard box and secure the lid. Cut a small hole in the side of the box and rest it on the kitchen window sill with the hole facing the window. Check the box regularly and water the mustard and cress seeds. What happens to the growing mustard and cress? Can you see the stems bend and lean towards the light coming through the hole?

eye brow

brow bone

eye socket

Seeing

We have five senses that help us to make sense of our world. We can taste and smell, hear noise, touch and see things around us. Seeing is the most important sense. The gift of sight helps us to find shelter, food and water, and to spot danger.

When our eyes are open, we see things because they *reflect* light, and the reflected light enters our eyes.

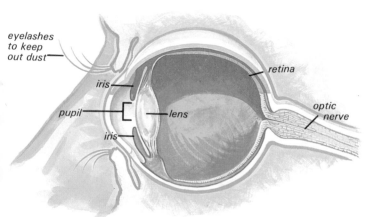

eyelashes
to keep
out dust

iris

pupil

iris

retina

lens

optic
nerve

Go into a darkened room and stare into a mirror. Look straight into your eyes. Light bounces back from the mirror and goes through the pupil. The pupil is really an opening which looks black because the inside of the eye is dark. As the room is darkened, the pupil opens wide to let in as much light as possible. Now open the curtains and stare into the mirror again. Can you see your pupil changing shape?

There is a screen at the back of your eye called the retina. An image of what you see is formed on this tiny screen. The retina is linked to the optic nerve which carries the message to the brain. The brain tells us what we are seeing. If the retina is damaged in an accident, then you could become blind or partially sighted.

As sight is vital, we need to take good care of our eyes. They are protected from bumps and knocks by eyelids and eyesockets, but remember, avoid looking directly at any very bright light and *never* look straight at the sun; the retina is very sensitive and could be damaged.

View of the eyes and the brain from underneath

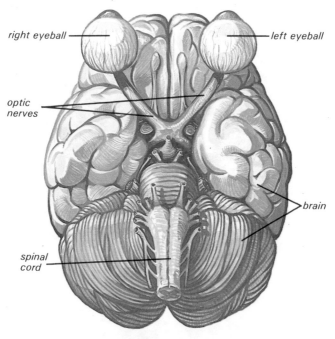

right eyeball — left eyeball

optic nerves

brain

spinal cord

Making a model eye

You can see how the eye works. Fill a small round clear glass bowl with cold tap water. Then pierce a small hole in a piece of black card (this represents the pupil in your eye). Firmly support a small candle on a piece of 'Plasticine' so that it will not fall over, and carefully light the wick. Switch off the lights and hold a piece of white card behind the bowl on the opposite side of the candle. This represents the retina. The candle light will pass through the hole in the card, through the bowl, and form an image on the white card. Move the card until you get a clear image of the candle. It will be small and upside down. The image on your retina is also upside down, but the brain interprets this and other information for us and tells us how big things are and how far away.

black card

inverted image

bowl of water

In a perfect model the white card would be stuck on the side of the bowl

candle

Eyes

Most human beings have binocular vision, which means that both eyes focus on an object and each retina sends to the brain a clear message of what that eye is seeing. Some people, though, have independent vision and they use each eye separately. Chameleons have revolving eyes to help them to spot insects. Fish that live on the ocean bed have eyes close together at the top of their heads so they can see what is happening above them.

Camels have an extra eyelid over each eye. The extra eyelid is very thin and transparent. It protects the camels' eyes from sand particles flying in the desert air. Flies, bees and other insects have compound eyes which have hundreds of minute lenses.

Seeing through things

Take your eyes from this page for a moment and look around you. What can you see? Most things you spot reflect light from the sun or from an electric light bulb. We can see clearly through some materials like glass and water. Materials that we can see right through are called *transparent*. Are there any transparent materials close to you now? How many can you see?

Other materials let light through them, but the light is scattered in all directions, so that the eye only sees a blurred and confused image. Frosted glass, thick polythene, fog, and some kinds of natural crystals like quartz, for example, are called *translucent* materials. Can you find any translucent objects? There is a good way to check whether or not materials are translucent. Shine a beam of light from a torch in a room with the curtains closed. Try the beam through a selection of things you think are translucent and look closely. Are they translucent? How do you know?

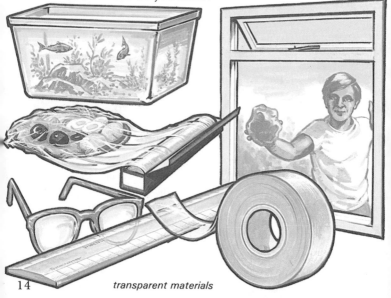

transparent materials

Most materials do not let light through at all, and they are called *opaque*. When sunlight or artificial light shines on an opaque material such as this page you are reading, nearly all the light is reflected back into the air, which means we can see it. Some of the light, though, is absorbed by the page and changed into heat. Don't worry — the page isn't going to burst into flame! The change in temperature is very, very small, but there certainly is a change that can be detected by a sensitive thermometer.

Shadows

shadow tig in the playground

Have you heard of Peter Pan? He is the central character in a famous children's book by J M Barrie. In the story, Peter Pan tries to get through the window of the Darling children, John, Wendy and Michael. Their nurse, a St Bernard dog called Nana, firmly closes the window and cuts off Peter Pan's shadow. Wendy feels sorry for poor Peter and sews back his shadow on his feet.

You can't cut your shadow off and have it sewn back in place, but you can have lots of fun playing with it. On a bright sunny day, play shadow games with a friend. Make interesting statue shapes with your body and ask your friend to draw round the outline with chalk. When the shape is drawn, leap out of the chalk outline and then see if you can fit back exactly.

Shadow tig is fun, too. Instead of catching each other, try standing on each other's shadow. Who can make the smallest body shadow? The biggest? The tallest? Think about shadows for a while. Do they always fall in the same direction? Look at something permanent outside your home, like a washing post or telegraph pole, and make a chalk mark where the shadow falls at 9 am. Where is the shadow at 10 am? Where will it be at midday? Can you make a shadow clock that tells the time?

The umbra and penumbra

Umbra is the Latin word for shadow. Umbra describes the darkest part of a shadow, and if you look at a ground shadow you will see it surrounded by a lighter outline. This lighter portion is called the *penumbra*. Penumbra is from two Latin words, paene and umbra, which means, almost a shadow. Can you make a shadow with a torch and outline the penumbra and umbra? We use the word umbra today. Umbrellas shade us from the sun, and Umbelliferae are umbrella-shaped plants, like cow parsley and hogweed, which shade smaller plants below.

Eclipse

Giant clouds throw big areas into shade as they pass between the land and the sun, blocking out light. There is a rock outcrop in Arizona so big that its shadow stretches for the enormous distance of 56km. Some great American skyscrapers cast long shadows, but they fall on other buildings so the true dimensions are difficult to measure. The longest and widest shadows are made in early morning and late afternoon. Why do you think this is so? What is the longest shadow you can find?

New York

When the Earth moves between the sun and the moon, it blocks sunlight. When this happens, the moon (which is about 380,000 km away) is plunged into darkness. This is called an eclipse of the moon. An eclipse of the sun occurs when the moon passes between it and the Earth. The moon's shadow falls on the Earth, casting large areas into shade.

You can see how an eclipse happens by using a table-tennis ball and a small electric lamp. Hold the ball (which is the moon) in front of the light bulb and bring the ball to about half a metre from one eye. Close the other eye. Now slowly move away from the bulb, keeping your eye closed, until the ball and the bulb appear to be about the same size. Then move the ball slowly across the light from the bulb. What happens? Can you see the light disappear? As you move the ball into line with the bulb, you *eclipse* light from your eye.

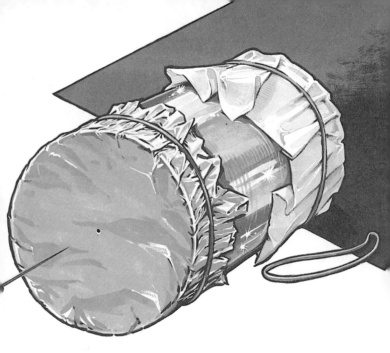

A pinhole viewer

Pinhole viewers have been made by amateur scientists for hundreds of years, because they demonstrate that light travels in straight lines. A model viewer is easy to build from junk material.

You will need an empty, clean tin can (a small baked bean size is ideal), a sheet of tracing paper, some elastic bands long enough to go round the tin, a pin, a sheet of tin foil and a sheet of black paper. Carefully use a tin opener to remove the closed end of the tin, making sure that the opener does not leave a dangerous jagged edge. You now have a tin without a top or bottom. Put the sheet of tin foil over the end and fix it to the tin with an elastic band. Then poke a small hole in the centre of the tin foil with the pin. Turn the tin over, and secure the

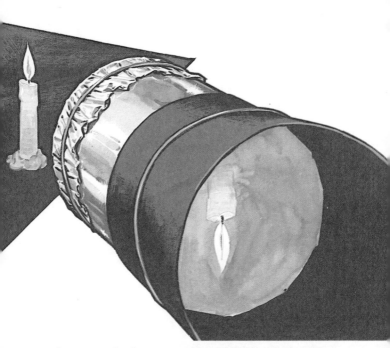

tracing paper in the same way to the other end. This is
the screen. The next stage is important to give you a good
picture. You are going to look through the viewer in
daylight, so you need to shade the screen by wrapping the
black paper round the end of the tin which has the
screen. Secure it with an elastic band. This adds to the
length of the viewer.

Try the viewer in a darkened area first, aiming the tin
at a bright object like a candle flame (be sure to fix the
candle rigidly in a saucer so that there is no danger of its
falling and setting something on fire). Look at the image
formed on the screen. Can you see the candle image?
What is unusual about it? The image is upside down,
because the rays of light travel in straight lines from the
top and bottom of the object being looked at, crossing as
they pass through the pinhole.

You can make a pinhole camera to take a black and white print. You need a small light-proof cardboard box (a shoe box is ideal), with a pinhole in the centre of one end. Then, in a darkened room, 'Sellotape' a piece of photographic paper inside the box, on the wall facing the pinhole. Hang a piece of card over the hole as a shutter, to block out the light from entering the pinhole at the wrong time. When you are ready, light the candle you used in the previous experiment, secure it directly in front of the pinhole, and remove the shutter for about ten minutes.

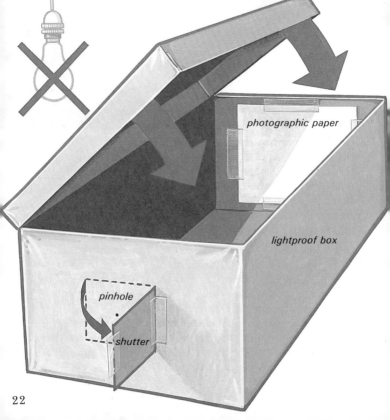

photographic paper

lightproof box

pinhole

shutter

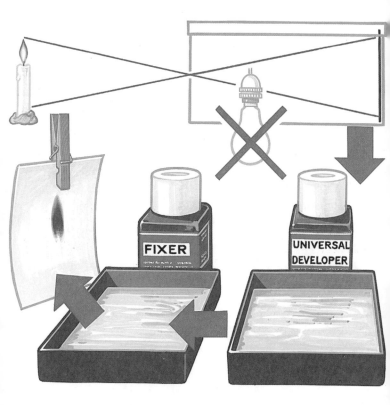

Photographic paper is sensitive to light, and changes colour when light rays touch its surface. The rest of the paper remains white. After ten minutes, remove the paper from the box. It needs developing and 'fixing' right away, otherwise it will turn dark purple. You can buy 'fixing' solution from a photographers' shop and, by following the instructions carefully, make your prints last for ever.

You may have to experiment with the exposure time, since the pinhole allows only a very small amount of light to enter the box. If you use a bigger hole, the exposure time will be reduced, but the pictures will be blurred.

Bending light

Light always travels in straight lines. If you go into the garden on a dark night and shine a torch, you can see a single beam of light. Another way to show that light travels in straight lines is to cut a piece of plastic garden hose about 2m in length, and ask a friend to hold one end. Pull the tubing taut, and look down the tube at your friend. Ask him to look through the other end. Can you see his eye? Now bend the tube in the middle and again look down it. Now what do you see? Why does this prove that light travels in straight lines?

Sometimes, though, light seems to break this rule. In 1621, a Dutch scientist called Willeboord Snell noticed that when light moves from air into water, the light bends. This strange but common effect is called *refraction*. Fill a glass with water and rest a straw in it.

Now look down at the straw as it enters the water. Can you see the straw appearing to bend? The light creates this strange phenomenon.

Now place a pebble in the bottom of an empty dish standing on a table. Keep your eye on the pebble and slowly move backwards until the pebble disappears from view. Now ask a friend to pour water slowly into the bowl. What happens? Can you see the pebble coming back into view? Why does this happen?

The light reflected from the pebble bends when water is poured into the bowl. So the pebble comes into view. Garden ponds and swimming pools never look as deep as they really are because of refraction. If someone in your home wears glasses, look at the line of his or her face where it appears to bend beneath the lenses.

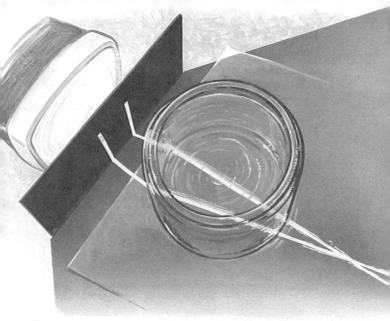

Lenses

Lenses are important. They are used in spectacles, microscopes, telescopes, projectors, cameras, and other optical instruments. The human eye has a lens. To understand how lenses work, fill a small jam jar with water, rest it on a sheet of white paper and add a few drops of milk with a straw. Then cut two slits in a card 2 cm apart and shine a torch towards them so that the rays of light pass through the slits. What happens to the rays as they pass through the jam jar? Can you see the light rays bend? The rays come together at the other side of the jar, meeting on the white card. This experiment works best in a darkened room.

You have made a water lens. The water lens forced the light rays to come together. This is called *convergence*, because the light rays converge on one another. Torch light bends in the same way through a bowl of water.

Some lenses are thicker at the centre than at the edges and these are called *convex* lenses. The water lens in the jam jar was a convex lens. Lenses that are thicker at the edges than in the middle are called *concave* lenses.

convex

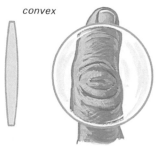

concave

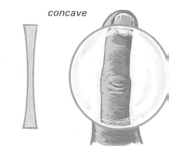

The burning glass

How could a goldfish bowl cause a fire? Mysterious fires in homes have been started by sunlight shining through a bowl of water (which is a convex lens) standing on window sills. The rays of light go through the bowl, converge, and meet at a point or *focus*, and produce heat. This can cause carpets or newspapers to smoulder, and burst into flames. All convex lenses can focus the rays of sunlight. Sometimes they are called burning glasses because they make things burn. Even discarded milk bottles in hedges and woods can start fires, because they act like a lens.

The magnifying glass

We now call burning glasses by another name. When you look through a burning glass the objects behind it seem to increase in size. They are *magnified* and we are looking through a *magnifying glass*.

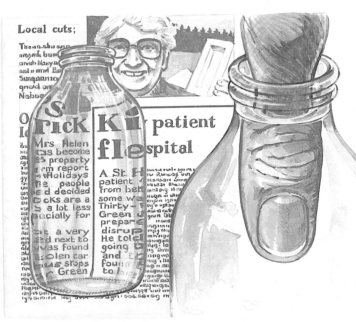

Making a magnifying glass is easy. Fill a milk bottle with tap water and hold a newspaper close to it. Look through the bottle at the newspaper. What do you see? Can you see how the print is enlarged? Can you guess how many times the print is magnified? Magnify your finger by putting it into the bottle of water. Can you see the large hairs on your finger? The water acts as a lens and magnifies the newspaper and your finger. Even little drops of water are small magnifying glasses.

Here is a way to make a water drop magnifier. Cut a round hole about the size of a fivepence coin in the middle of a piece of cardboard and tape some clear waterproof tape over the hole. Carefully, using a straw dropper, drop a small amount of water on the tape. The water does not wet the waterproof tape and it forms a small round lens. Look through the lens at a leaf and you will see the structure and detail quite clearly.

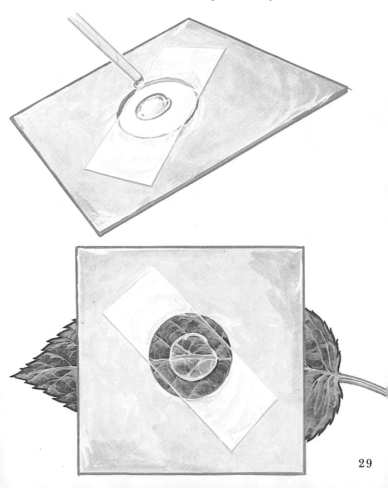

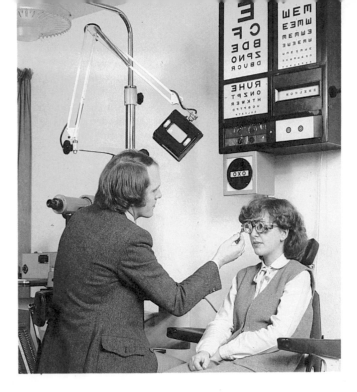

Spectacles

When you have your eyes tested at school by the doctor, you are asked to read out letters printed on a chart. The size of the letters gets smaller as you read down the card. If you have problems reading any of the letters on the card, the doctor will suggest you visit an ophthalmic optician, who will first make sure that your eyes are healthy. He will then examine them to determine whether spectacles may improve your vision. If you need spectacles, he will make a pair just for you, solving your eye problem. If your vision is the result of a squint or a lazy eye, he may also prescribe exercises.

If you are long-sighted, you can see things in the distance more clearly than objects close to your face. This problem is caused by light focusing beyond the retina in your eye. Convex lenses will correct this problem. Some people are short-sighted, and distant objects appear fuzzy and out of focus because light is focused in front of the retina. To correct this condition, concave lenses are fitted to the spectacles.

Another error of vision is called *astigmatism*, which is due to an irregularity within the eye: this can also be corrected by special lenses.

Glasses were invented a long time ago. We do not know who first thought of the idea of making glasses to wear, but we do know that Galileo (1564-1642), a renowned thinker and scientist, made a pair for himself when his eyesight began to fade.

detail from 'The Adoration of the Kings' (1564)
by Pieter Brueghel the Elder

Rainbows

Rainbows have always been thought of as magical and special.

They are magnificent arcs of colour hanging in the sky. When sunlight shines on falling raindrops a band of seven colours appears. Sunlight is not pure. Different colours make up sunlight and they are: red, orange, yellow, green, blue, indigo and violet. You can remember these colours easily if you use a sentence to help you. *Richard of York gave battle in vain*. The first letter from each word is the same as in each colour. These seven colours are known as the spectrum. Usually on a sunny but rainy day one rainbow is visible in the sky. This is the primary rainbow. Sometimes a second and fainter rainbow can be seen with the colours in the reverse order. This is the secondary rainbow.

When you are washing up the dishes in the sink, look at the soap bubbles. Sometimes you will see rainbow colours on the bubbles. Blow some bubbles and see if you can make floating rainbows.

You can make a rainbow. You need a prism, a sheet of white card or paper, and sunlight. Hold the prism so that the sunlight passes straight through it. A spectrum will appear on the card if you hold it close to the prism. Don't worry if you don't have a prism. Stand a small mirror in a dish full of water and rest it on the window sill that gets the most sunlight. The water will break up the white light, and if you juggle the mirror around, it will catch the colours and send them onto a wall or small screen made from card or paper. Sometimes water spray from a lawn sprinkler will produce a rainbow. On a sunny day, try it and see.

The spectrum

A farmer's son from Lincolnshire, Sir Isaac Newton (1642-1727), was the first scientist to show that white light is made of seven different colours. He directed a beam of light through a glass prism and produced the spectrum. He also reversed the prism effect. He cut out a disc and painted the seven spectrum colours on it in equal amounts. When he rotated the card, the seven colours merged to form white.

You can do this. Cut a piece of card into a circle about the size of a small tin lid, paint the seven spectrum colours on it, then make a hole in the middle. Thread a loop of string through the hole, tie the ends and put your hands into the loop at each side. Turn the disc as quickly as you can until all the string is twisted. Pull outwards with each hand and the disc will spin freely. Watch the colours combine to make white.

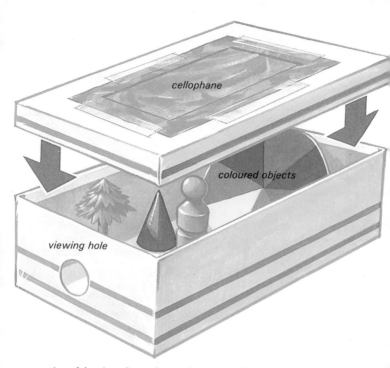

cellophane

coloured objects

viewing hole

An object's colour depends upon which part of the spectrum it reflects. A red pen looks red because it reflects light from the red part of the spectrum and absorbs the rest. But if we looked at the red pen in a beam of light that didn't have any red in it, the pen would look black because it cannot reflect the other spectrum colours.

Sweets are often wrapped in transparent cellophane paper. Collect some wrappings and make a viewing box similar to the one in the picture. Put a blue wrapping over the hole and put the box near a light. Look through the viewing hole and you will see a blue shadow inside the box. Now put some coloured objects inside and look through the viewer. What can you see? What effect does the blue light have on the colours in the box?

Mixing colours

warm harmonious colours

In painting, artists use a Colour Wheel to make exciting and interesting pictures. The colours are divided into two groups: warm colours which are red, orange and yellow, and cold colours: blue, green and purple.

Colours opposite to each other on the wheel are *complementary* colours. When complementary colours are placed side by side, they look brighter.

cold harmonious colours

When you want orange to look really deep, paint something blue next to it. To show an intense bright red, match it with green. If you want a room to look restful and soothing, the wallpaper should be in blue, green or purple. If you want an active room, use warm reds, orange and yellow.

Draw a similar picture on two sheets of paper. Colour one of the pictures in felt pen or paint and use green, blue and purple. Then colour the other picture in red, yellow and orange. When they dry, stand back and look at them both. Can you notice the mood and atmosphere they produce? Now on a white sheet of paper, pin a small square of orange or red. Stare at it for about a minute. Remove the colour and then stare at the paper. Can you see the complementary colour appearing very faintly where the bright colour was pinned? Why do you think this happens?

Coloured lights

Theatres use spotlights with colour filters to produce

lighting at the Young Vic theatre

different stage effects. These shine on the players so that they can be clearly seen by the audience. Other spotlights hang from the walls and ceiling of the theatre and light the action around the stage. Colour filters are used to produce interesting effects. Red or yellow filters are used for sunny scenes, blue or green filters for cold and night scenes. Sometimes two separate spotlights of different colours are focused on the same place to produce a new colour.

Mirrors

When you comb your hair in front of a mirror, you see yourself because the mirror throws back the light. The light is *reflected*. Because the mirror surface is highly polished, the image is a perfect representation of you. If the surface was not polished or smooth, light would get reflected in all directions.

Have you played 'chase the light spot'? Use a small mirror to reflect a spot of light on a wall. Turn the mirror slightly, and the direction of the reflected rays changes, and the spot moves. Can a friend with another small mirror catch your spot? What happens if you use two mirrors each?

Because light can be reflected in this way, you can use mirrors to see round corners. This is how a periscope works. You can make one with two small mirrors and a 30 cm ruler. Secure the mirrors at the ends of the ruler with a lump of 'Plasticine', and tilt them at a slight angle.

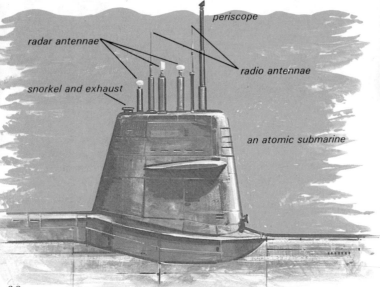

periscope

radar antennae

radio antennae

snorkel and exhaust

an atomic submarine

Move behind a cupboard or a sofa, kneel down and look through the periscope. Move the mirrors until you can see over the furniture. Light reflected from objects in the room strikes the top mirror and is reflected to your eyes. The commander of a submarine relies on his periscope. It is the all-seeing eye of the underwater craft, and sees what is happening on the surface.

Now you know how to make a simple periscope, design one, from a cardboard tube, that you could use at a football or netball match. Can you make something to see round corners?

Can you use two mirrors to see the back of your head? What happens when you hold some writing in front of a mirror? Can *you* do some mirror writing?

More work with mirrors

Stand two small mirrors at an angle to each other, so that their sides are touching. Put a plastic toy between them, and look into the mirrors. How many images of the toy can you see? If you change the angle of the mirrors, do you see more or fewer images? When we use two mirrors like this, we get images of images. As you close the mirrors, the number of images grows.

Stand two mirrors about 30 cm apart and turn them so that they face each other. Place a toy soldier or something similar between the two mirrors. Look over the top of one of the mirrors into the other. What can you see? Can you see a line of toy soldiers going away from you? These are the images of the image of the soldier.

kaleidoscope

Now tape three small mirrors together and rest them on a sheet of white card. Drop some coloured beads in the space between the mirrors. Look down at the reflections

40

of the beads. What do you see? Move the beads and you get a different pattern. This is a *kaleidoscope*.

If a mirror surface is curved, the eye sees strange and amusing images. Look at the images in a soup spoon. What is the difference between the image in the front of the spoon and that seen on the back? Look at the reflections in metal teapots and anything else that has a round, polished surface. Funfairs often have collections of curved mirrors that form curious images of our bodies.

concave shaving mirror

Making a telescope

We can see lots of stars at night, twinkling in the sky, sending out light that eventually reaches Earth. We get a good view of the moon because it reflects the light from the sun. Many people, especially astronomers who study the sun, moon and stars, want a better view of the skies and use a *telescope*. This is an instrument which appears to bring things closer.

Some telescopes are called *refractors* because they use lenses which *refract* or bend light. There are other telescopes which use small curved mirrors instead of lenses. Sir Isaac Newton made the first *reflecting* telescope about three hundred years ago. The curved mirrors do not bend the light rays but reflect them and, like the lenses, gather them at a focal point. The image is magnified by an eye-piece. When you use a telescope of this type you look into the side of it, instead of directly into the telescope.

the Hale reflector telescope
at Mount Palomar, California, USA

You can make a simple reflecting telescope with a small concave mirror (a shaving mirror is ideal), a small magnifying lens and a handbag mirror. Stand the shaving mirror on a window sill, pointing it towards the stars. Hold the small mirror so that you can just see a reflection of the shaving mirror in the middle. Use a magnifying glass to look at the reflection. You have now made a reflecting Newtonian telescope.

The largest reflecting telescope in the world has a mirror 5m wide. This is the Hale Reflector Telescope at Palomar in the United States. Reflecting telescopes are easier to make than refracting telescopes because of the problem of making huge, perfect lenses.

If you buy a telescope from a shop, remember you must *never* look at the sun through it. You could hurt your eyes so badly that your sight would be permanently damaged. Telescopes are for land objects, or night-time viewing of the moon and stars.

Optical illusions

Sometimes sunlight plays tricks with our eyes. Things are not always what they appear to be. Desert travellers sometimes mistakenly think they see palm trees and water in the distance. This is a *mirage*, an optical illusion caused by unequal heating of the air, resulting in the bending of light rays. What the travellers actually see is the vision of palm trees and water which is a long distance off beyond the horizon.

Concorde takes off — note the optical illusion in the upside down image

You can make your own optical illusions. Get an old telephone directory and draw a felt pen spot on the top right hand corner of page one. On the following pages, in the same position on the sheet, draw more spots, each one bigger than the one before. Now flick the pages and watch the spot grow in size.

Make a small booklet of about twenty pages and staple at the centre fold. Place a sheet of carbon paper between the pages. On a separate piece of paper draw the body of a pinman. Put this on top of the booklet and draw firmly over the body, the head and the limbs. Take out the carbon sheet and work through the pages, draw in the head and limbs, making each shape slightly different. Now flick through the booklet and watch the pinman move. The images overlap and the drawings appear to move.

Animated cartoons are not moving films but thousands of drawings, each one slightly different from the previous one. When moved in sequence, they look as if they are alive. Famous cartoons like Tom and Jerry, Mickey Mouse, Donald Duck and others are made this way. About twenty five different pictures are shown every second, and we think we see a continuous movement.

Living without light

We know that if the sun exploded and disintegrated, life on Earth would perish. Light and heat are fundamental to our survival. Yet, some plants and animals do live without any light from the sun ever reaching them.

When they make food, plants use the green chlorophyll in their leaves. Some plants do not have chlorophyll, and are not green in colour. They cannot make their own food, but feed off other plants and decaying animals. The most well known are fungi and moulds that we see in woods during the warm autumn months, and growing on jam and sometimes old shoes lying in cupboards in our homes. These plants grow well in complete darkness. Put a squashed tomato in a bag and hide it in a box for a few days. It soon gets covered with microscopic moulds.

Animals that live underground generally do not require light from the sun. Some of them do not have eyes, especially the earthworm, whilst others have very weak eyesight, like the mole and the badger. Woodlice, centipedes and millipedes have no eyes at all, and if uncovered will quickly scurry away to the darkness. Leeches and other water worms are sightless, and sea creatures like mussels, oysters and scallops survive without seeing.

woodlouse

47

Laser beams

Light has incredible energy. When you switch on a light, the light streams in all directions from the bulb, illuminating a room. Light from an instrument called a *laser* goes in one direction only. A huge amount of energy is produced from a laser. The beam is so intense it can cut holes in steel sheets 3 cm thick.

a laser cutting tool

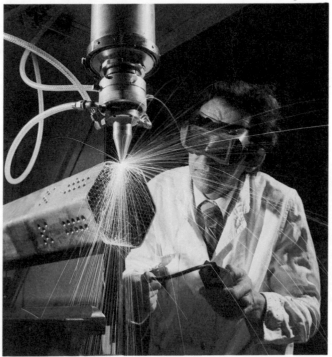

A laser beam is very narrow. The instrument is used in industry to melt and weld together very tiny parts of machinery. Surgeons are using laser beams in delicate surgery to burn away diseased cells without damaging other parts of the body. In 1962, a laser beam was directed at the moon. The beam of light was so bright that scientists saw the reflection just over two seconds later. This experiment led to other investigations to find out how useful lasers could be in space research. They could be used for sending messages to other planets and for communication between Earth and manned spacecraft. Future astronauts circling distant planets would be able to quickly pick up news and orders from space stations on Earth. In 1967, French scientists launched two satellites equipped with laser reflectors. They were easily tracked by laser beams from control stations in France. They are instruments for the future, and may in time to come, even help us to exchange information with possible life forms on distant planets.

optical fibres using light instead of electricity are now being used to carry telephone calls. The initial power source is an 0.5 laser beam

Solar energy

The sun is a source of energy we can always rely on. Now that other forms of fuel are getting more expensive as the supplies dwindle, many scientists are investigating ways of collecting and using the sun's energy.

Solar cells are a recent invention. They absorb the sun's energy and change it into electricity. This technique is used in many satellites that circle the Earth on scientific missions. The problem with solar cells, though, is that they are too expensive to make at the moment to use as a power source in our homes.

The Focusing Solar Collector concentrates the sun's energy by reflecting its rays to a single and powerful point. This produces intense heat. Scientists have made a huge solar furnace from a solar collector in France which produces a temperature of more than 3,300 degrees Celsius. In the furnace the power from the light rays melts steel 1 cm thick in less than a minute.

focusing solar collector

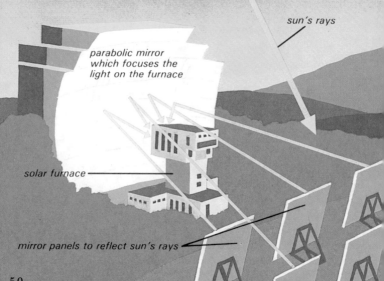

sun's rays

parabolic mirror which focuses the light on the furnace

solar furnace —————

mirror panels to reflect sun's rays

The Flat Plate Solar Collector is used for heating homes. The plate is a collection of long thin metal pipes that carry air or water. The collector is placed on the rooftop of a home so that it faces south and catches all the available sunlight. The sun warms up the air or water and this circulates through pipes around the building, taking warmth to every room. If the collector uses water, a solution of antifreeze is added so that the water does not freeze during cold winter nights.

If this system of heating buildings is as successful as the scientists claim, then the sun will help mankind to get over the fuel shortage that is threatening all industrial nations at the present time.

flat plate solar collector

INDEX